Trick or treat?

Guide the trick-or-treaters through town. You must visit every house, but you can't use the same path more than once.

Haunted house

Color the picture.

Find the one that looks like this.

GLOW IN THE DARK

Happy Halloween!

Have fun completing the spook-tastic activities in this book.

Turn the page to escape a zombie swamp, search for witches, and puzzle over vampires.

Then press out and create Halloween crafts. You can use your glow-in-the-dark puffy stickers to finish the press-out pieces or wherever you want!

make believe ideas

Pick a pumpkin

Draw scary faces on the pumpkins to finish the decorations.

Here are some ideas for you to choose from:
eyes
noses
mouths

Circle four bats.

Mummy mix-up

Follow the lines to discover which mummy owns each jewel. Write the letters in the circles.

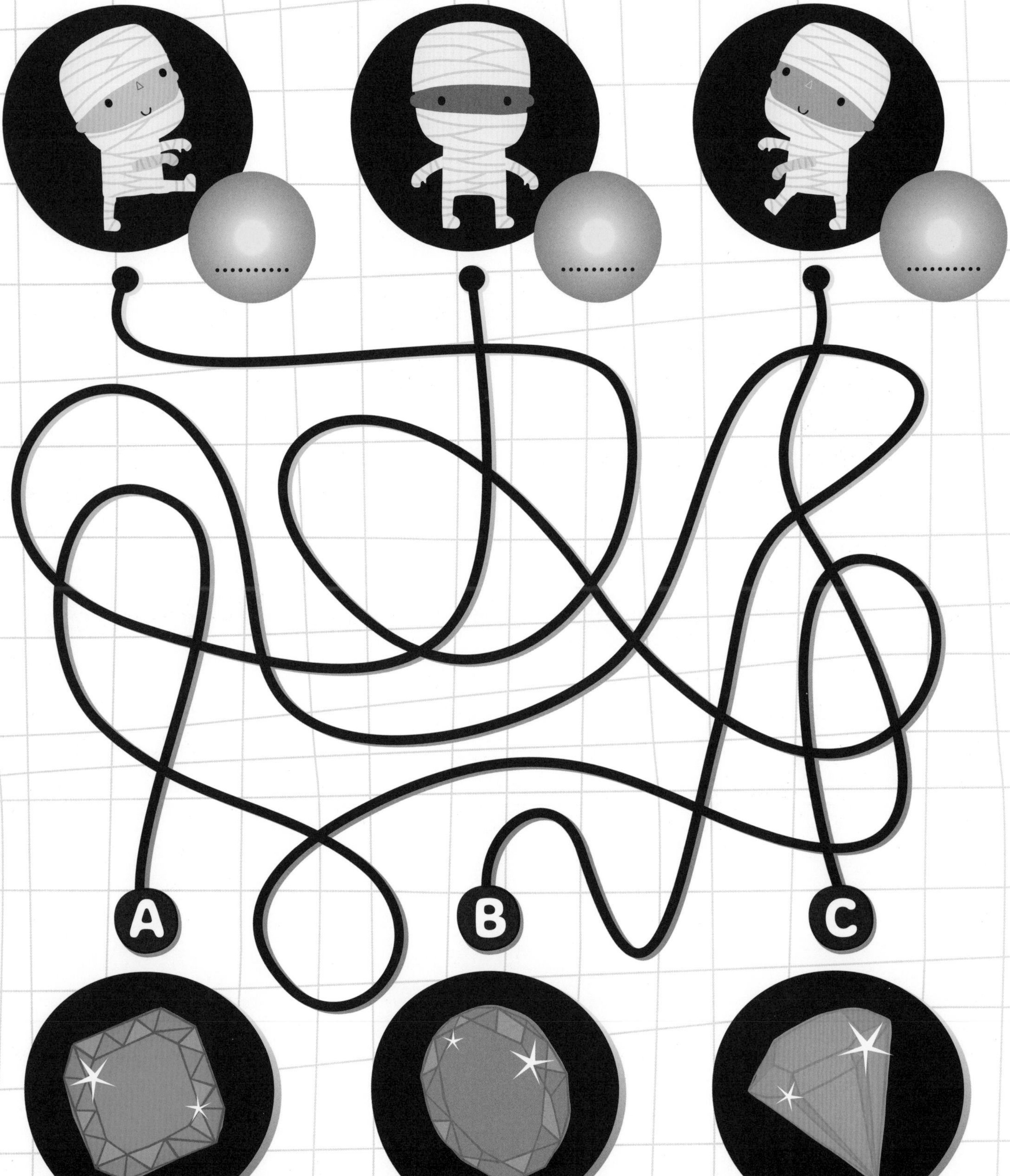

Creepy creatures

Unscramble the words. Use the pictures to guide you.

Halloween party

Search the scene for the things below.

How many can you see?
Write the answers in the circles.

1 .... ghost

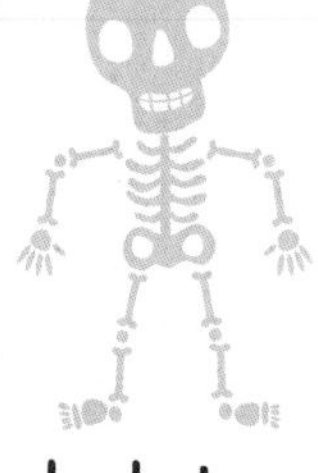

.... skeletons

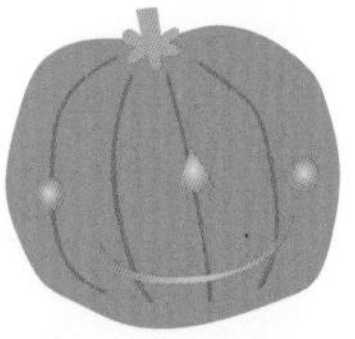

.... pumpkins

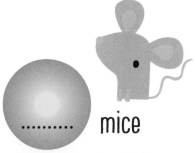

.... cupcakes

.... mice

.... spiders

Petrifying pairs

Draw lines to match the monster pairs.
Which monster doesn't have a partner?

Colorful skeletons

Trace the lines of the skull. Then color it.

Find the one that looks like this.

Foul food

Circle the thing that doesn't belong on each shelf.

Doodle designs to finish the cookies.

Count the treats in each jar. Then circle the answer.

1 2 3 4 5

4 5 6 7 8

6 7 8 9 10

Use color to make the pictures match.

Wonderful Wizards

Find and circle ten differences between the scenes.

Check the boxes when you find them.

1 2 3 4 5 6 7 8 9 10

Monster mash

Color the picture. Use the key to guide you.

1 2 3 4 5 6 7 8

Vampire watch

Circle **true** for the things that are in the picture.
Circle **false** for the things that are not in the picture.

There are three vampires.	True	False
There are two ghosts.	True	False
The bat is black.	True	False

All Hallows Eve

Use color to finish the patterns on each row.

Zombie swamp

Guide the zombie through the swamp. Use the key to guide you.

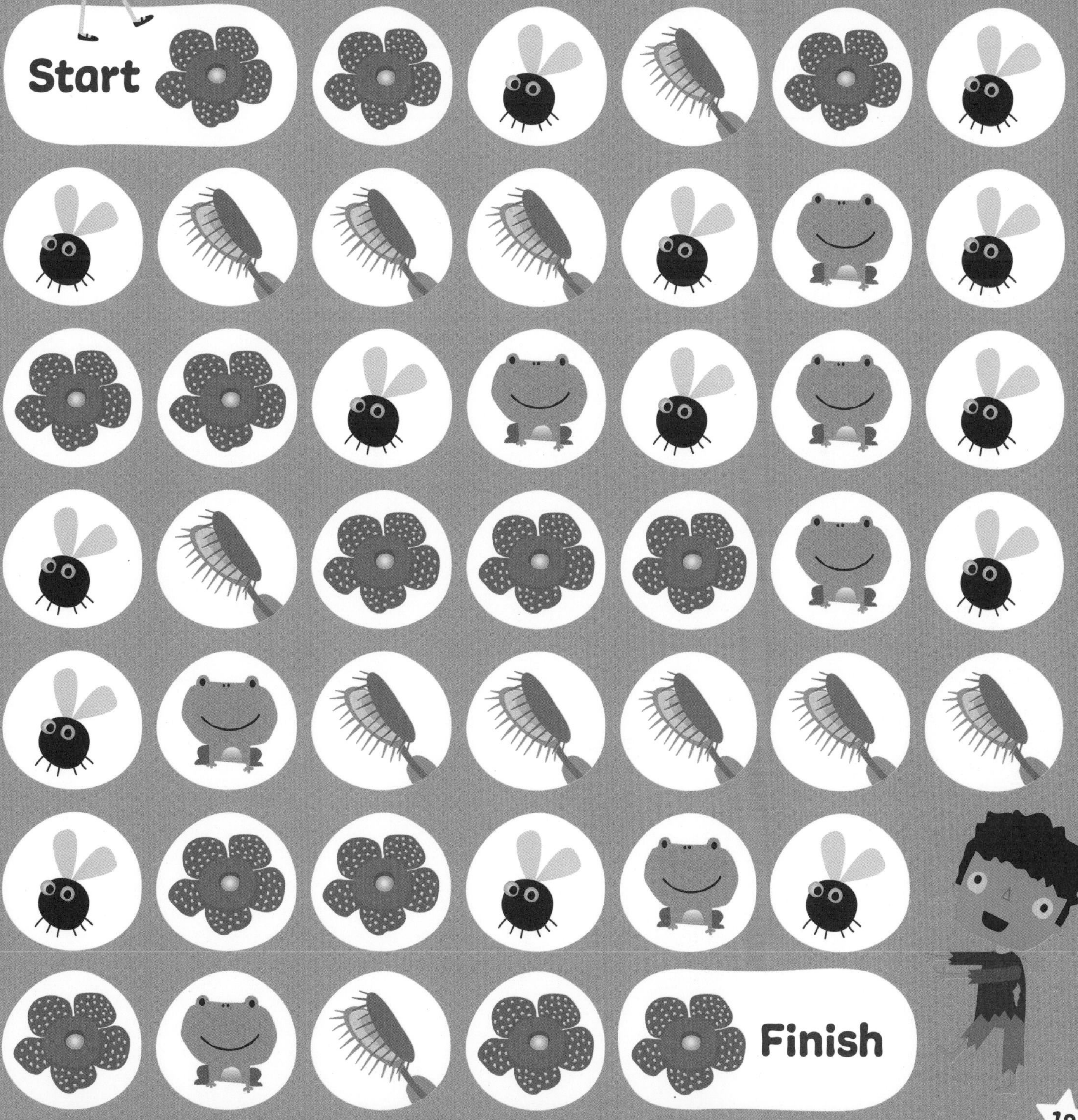

Wicked werewolves

Draw lines to connect the close-ups with the correct werewolf.

Search the grid for the words below. Words can go across or down.

- claw
- howl
- moon
- tail
- teeth
- wolf

t	r	s	f	z	h	q	e
e	i	e	z	i	o	p	t
e	l	c	l	a	w	o	m
t	p	z	i	j	l	u	o
h	a	w	o	l	f	z	o
r	x	n	u	o	v	q	n
u	t	a	i	l	t	w	x
q	d	e	c	a	n	m	z

Are there more trick-or-treaters or wolves?

Terrible tombs

Search the grid for the patterns below.
Check the boxes when you find them.

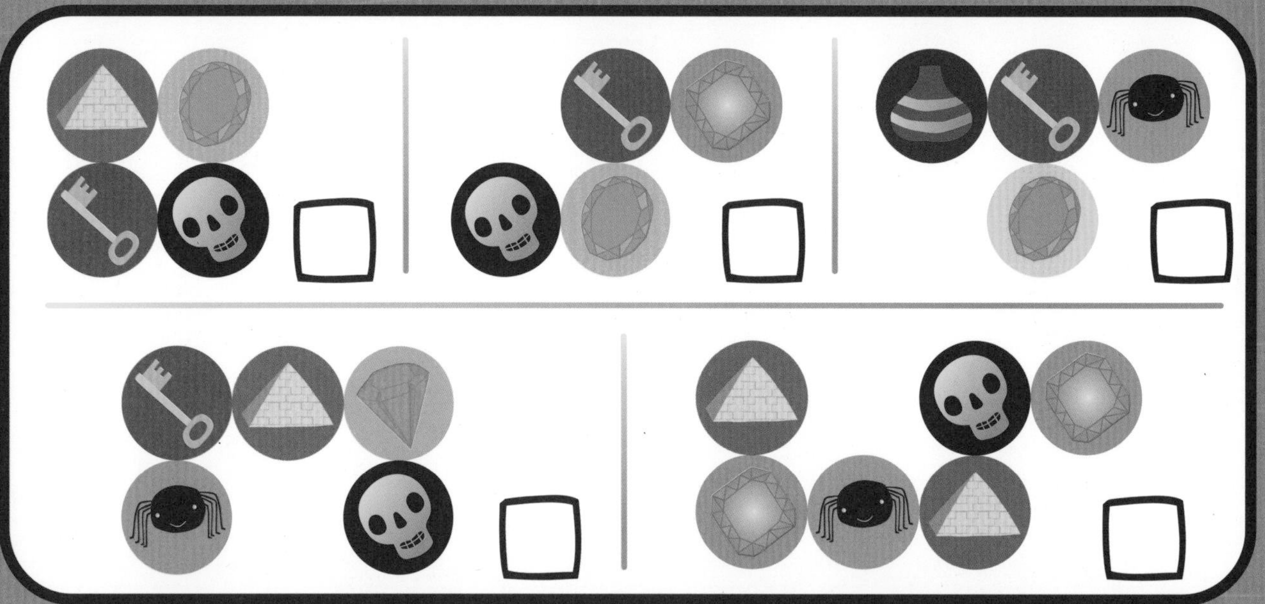

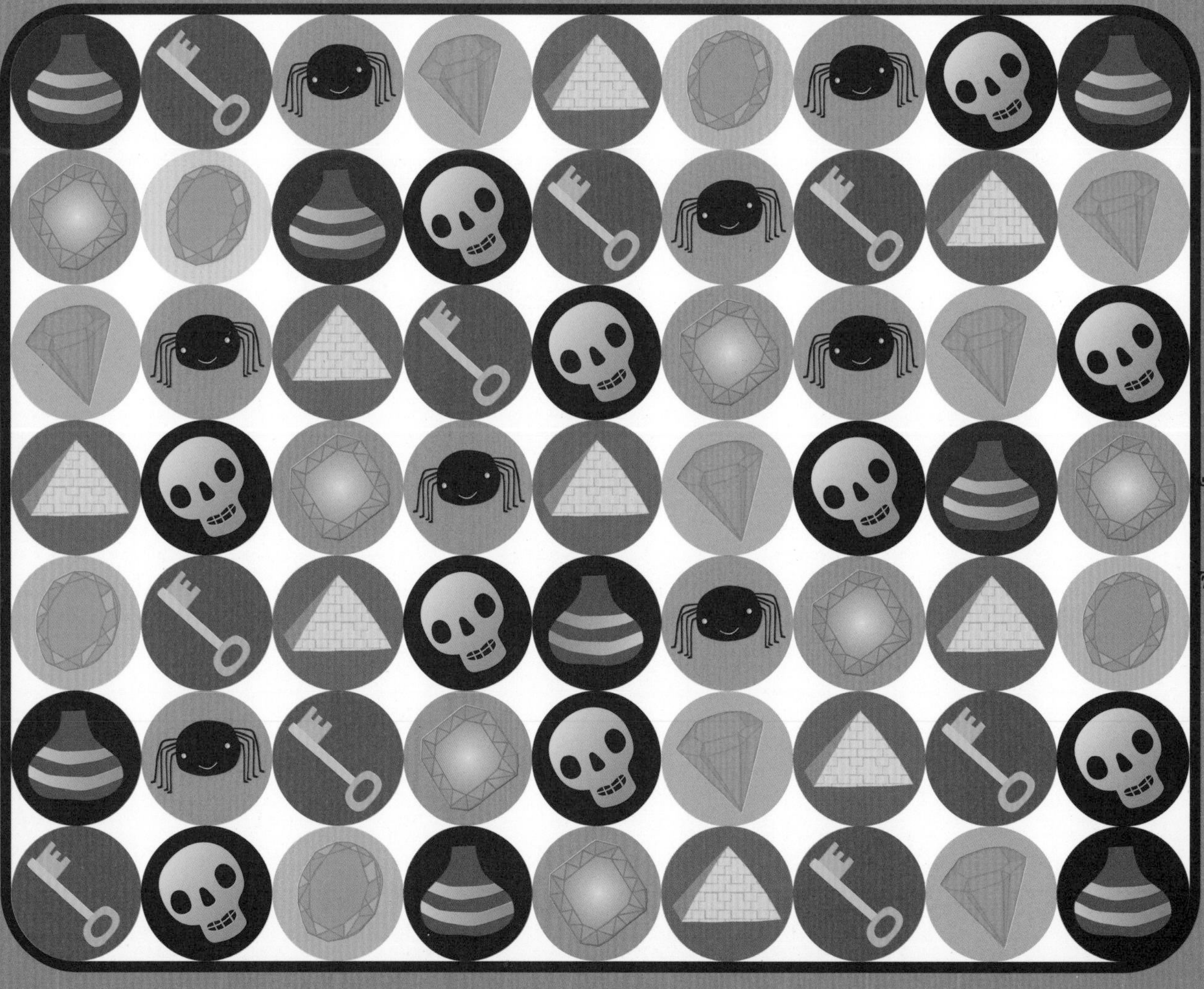

Scary scribbles

Join the dots to finish the ghost.

How many spiders can you count? ....

Quick quiz

Circle the pictures to answer the questions below.

Who is the smallest?

Who is eating a cupcake?

Who has green skin?

Who is wearing a witch's hat?

Who is holding a broom?

Who has glasses?

Forest frights

Find and color...

the spiders in **blue**.

the frogs in **green**.

the bats in **purple**.

the owls in **orange**.

Circle the one that matches this silhouette.

Which witch?

Look at the clues, and then search the page for the witch.

The witch has these things:

black and purple hat + broom + glasses

In the shadows

Which row of silhouettes matches the creatures below?

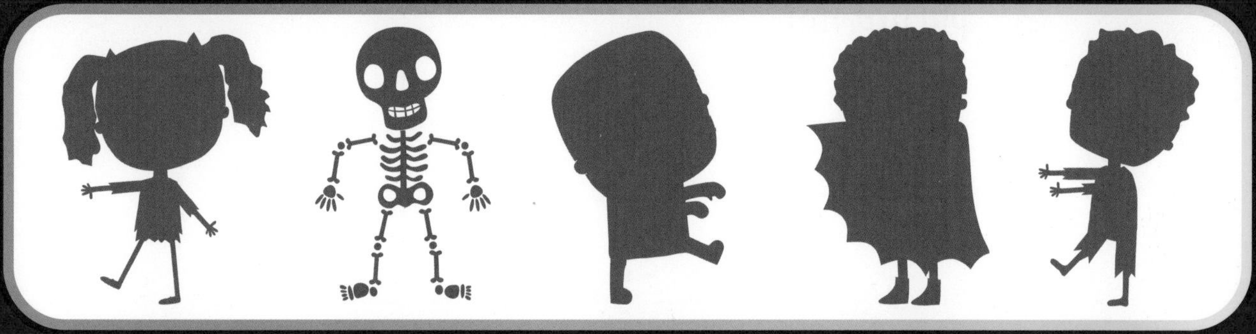

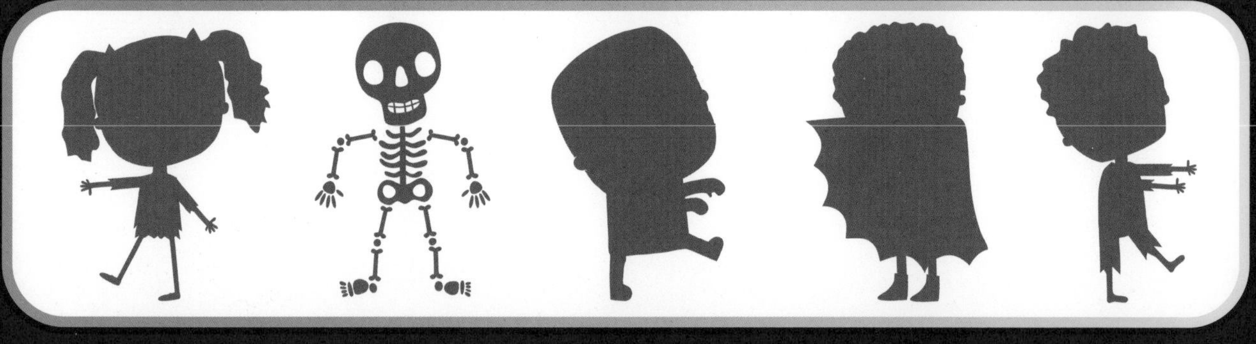

Spooky street

Use doodles and color to finish the haunted house.

Answer for page 31: The spookiest house is B.

Finish the sums to see whose house is the spookiest.
Use the key to solve the sums.

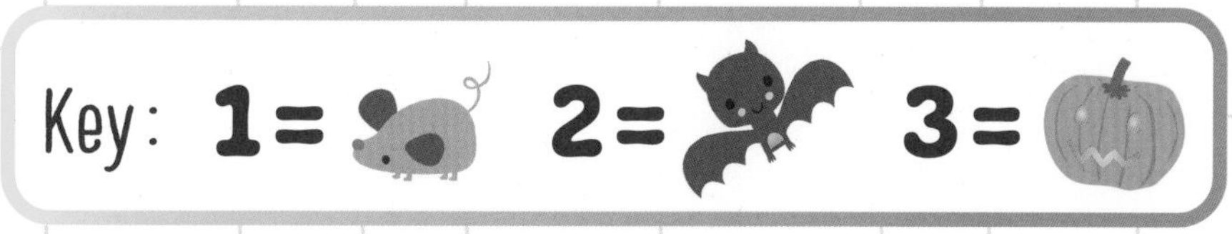

Which house is the spookiest? Write the answer.

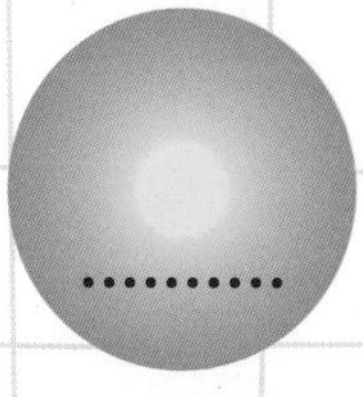

Circle five differences between the pictures.

Happy Halloween!

Color the picture. Use the dots to guide you.

SPOOKY WEB

1. Press out the web template, the hole in the middle, and the small holes around the outside.
2. Ask an adult to cut some string and tie a knot at one end.
3. Thread the string through a small hole and pull until the knot holds the string in place.
4. Then thread the string across the central hole and into any other small hole you want.
5. Keep going until you've used all the holes and have created a spooky web!
6. Press out the spiders and flies and slot them through the string to finish.

TIP!

When you've finished your spooky web, thread some ribbon through the hole at the top and hang it wherever you want.

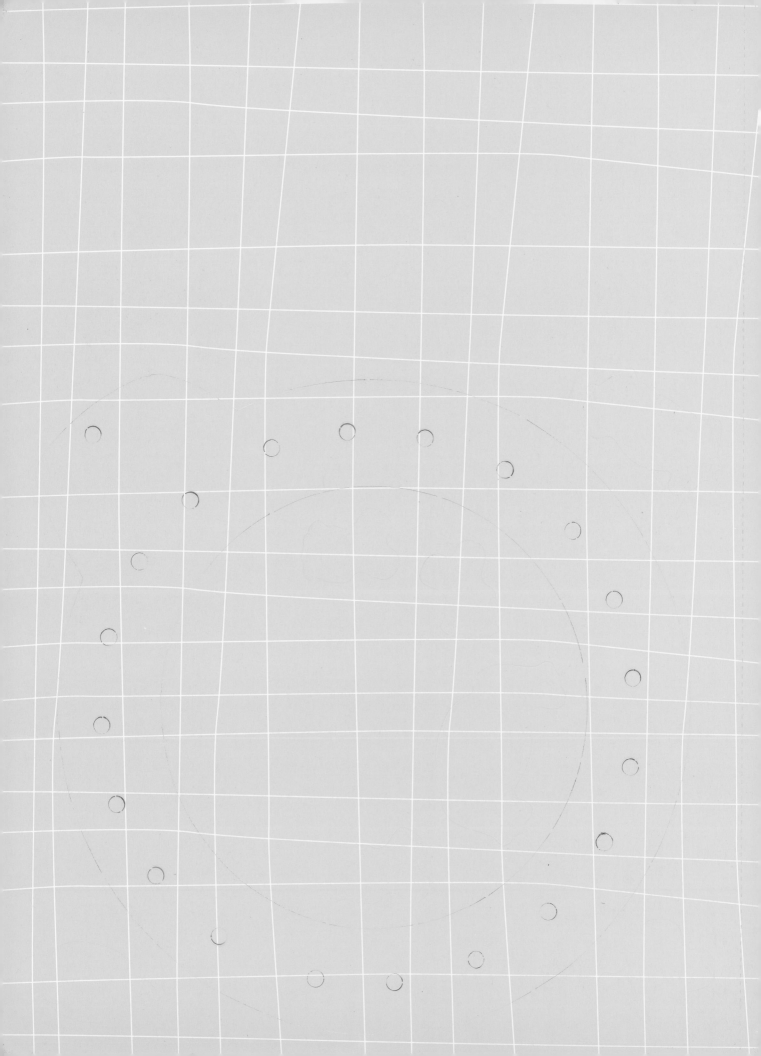

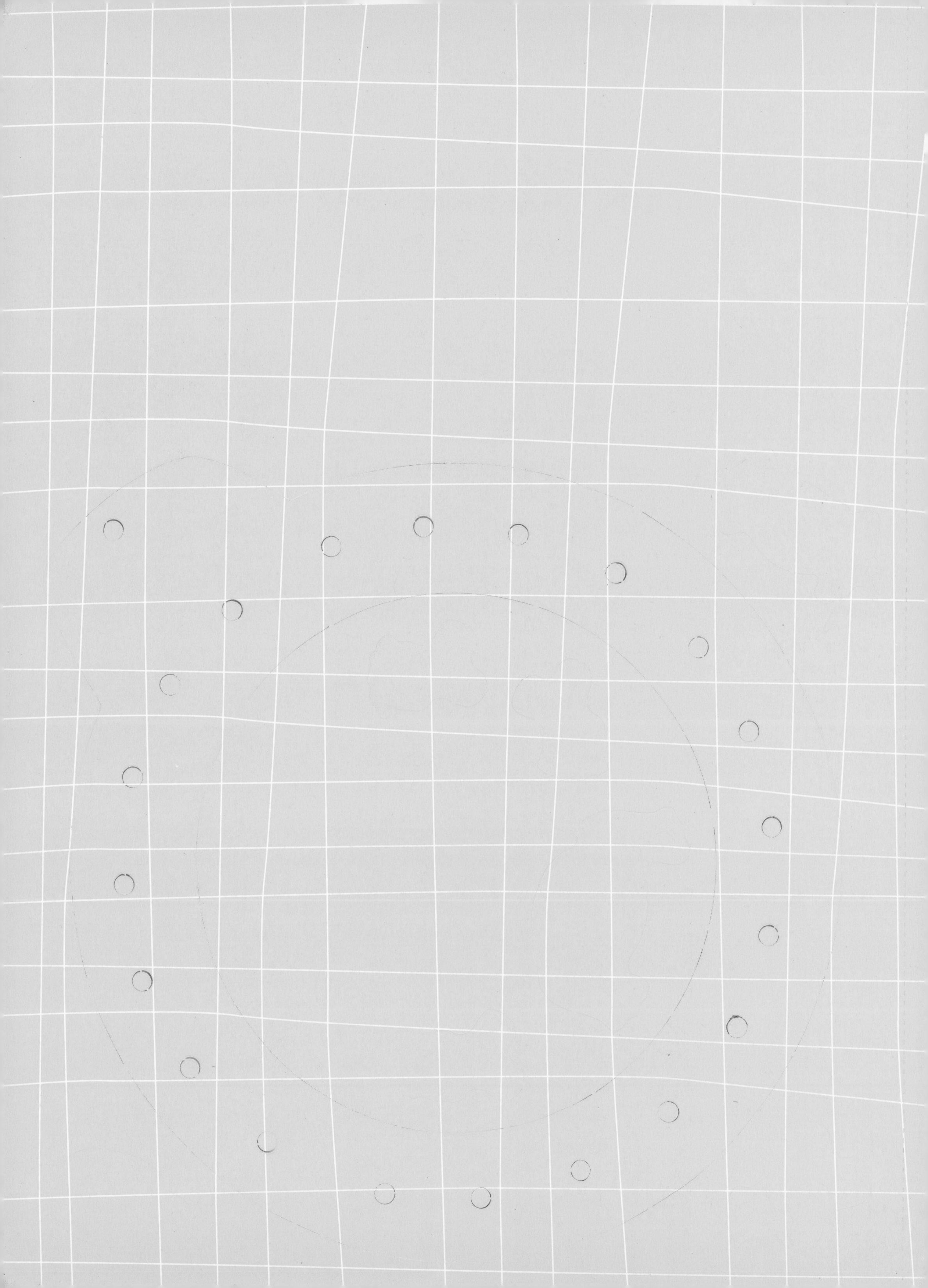

BOO-TIFUL BUNTING

Press out the shapes and fold along the creases.
Tape the folded part down over some ribbon,
and then hang the bunting wherever you want.

DARE TO PAIR

A fun game for 2 to 4 players!

1. Press out the cards and arrange them picture-side down.
2. Players take turns turning over two cards. If the cards match, set them aside. If they do not match, return them picture-side down.
3. Keep going until you have found all the pairs. The winner is the one with the most pairs at the end of the game!

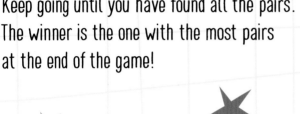

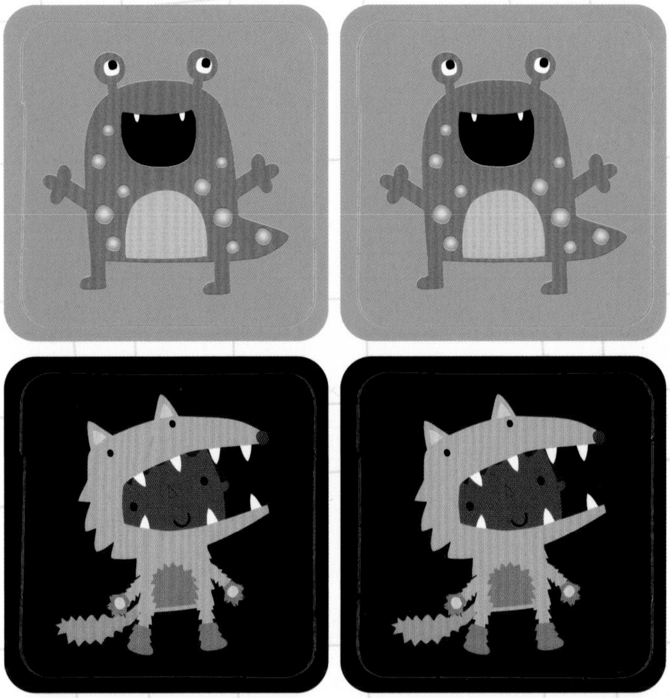

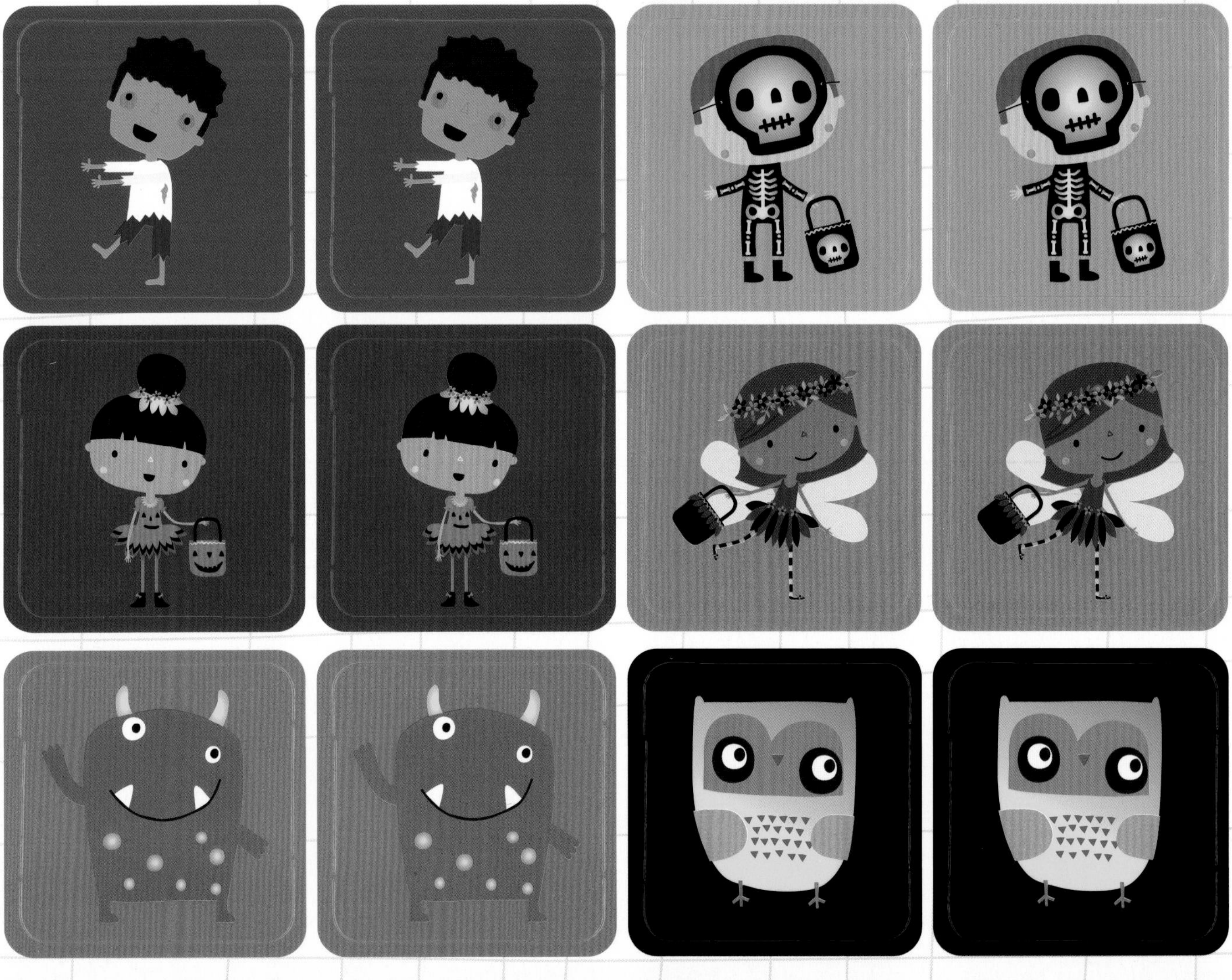